May 11, 1992

Christopher Ryan Davis —

We love you
see you in OZ!!!

Roger S. Baum

THE Silly OZbul OF OZ and Toto

ROGER S. BAUM

ILLUSTRATED BY LISA MERTINS

Yellow Brick Road
Publishers, Inc.
California

Dorothy packs her finest dress for the Wizard's birthday party.

"Please be good while I'm away. I'll be back very soon," assures Dorothy.

Dorothy says, "good-bye" to the SillyOZbul and Toto from atop the speedy Sawhorse.

Dorothy is gone. They wished it was possible for them to go to the surprise birthday party. It wasn't long before the SillyOZbul and Toto decide to travel to Glinda's Palace on their own.

. . . And they will bring along some birthday cookies for the Wizard.

Off they go.

The SillyOZbul accidentally drops the Wizard's birthday cookies.
Down a hill they fall, ribbon and all.

Toto and the SillyOZbul attempt to grab the cookies. Instead, they fall too. Over and over. Down the hill they tumble.

Wouldn't you know it, at the bottom of the hill is a beehive.
The bees and their Queen are very unhappy.

Toto quickly grabs the cookie bag. They run and hop as fast as they can.

Into a nearby stream they jump. The bees will not follow them here.
The SillyOZbul keeps the Wizard's birthday cookies high and dry.

On their way again. But, it's late and it will be dark soon.

SillyOZbul of OZ and Toto

It is a cold and lonely night.

It's sunrise. They better get going. Glinda's Palace is still a long way off.

Oh no! It begins to rain. They find a nearby cave
for shelter. It looks like something else
is using the cave for shelter too.

They cannot wait any longer for the rain to stop or they will be late for the Wizard's surprise birthday party. It's cold, wet and muddy.

They'll chance it, rain and all, and hope Glinda's Palace is nearby.

They made it!

Dorothy scolds them, "Look how dirty and wet you are! But, I love you.
I'm glad you're here with us safe and sound. By-the-way," Dorothy smiled,
"You didn't miss the Wizard's birthday party."

The SillyOZbul hands Glinda the birthday cookies.

"Happy Birthday. Happy Ninety-second Birthday, Wizard," everyone yelled.

It was a wonderful surprise birthday party.

P.S. The Wizard's birthday cookies were delicious down to the last crumb.